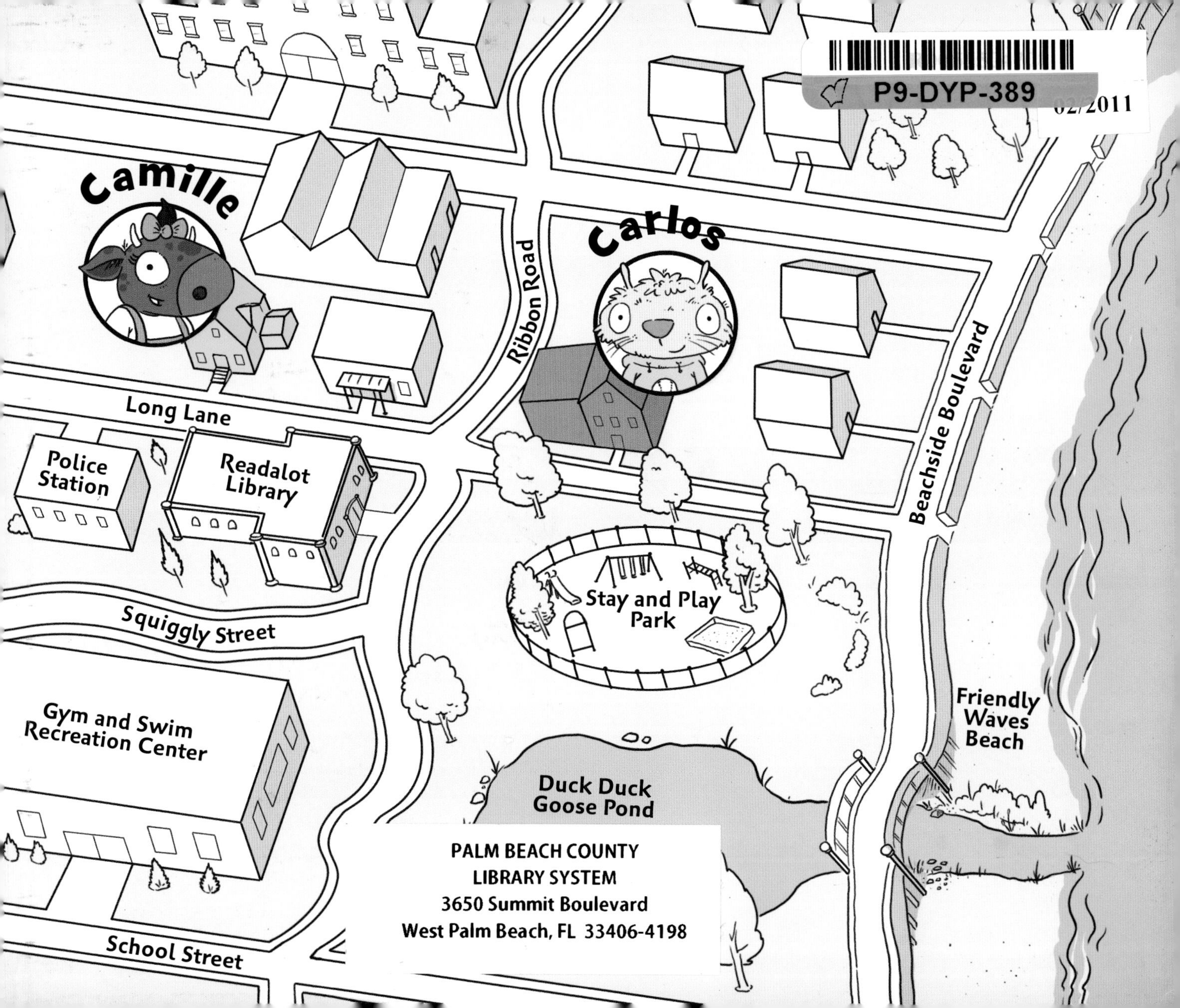
Camille
Carlos
Ribbon Road
Long Lane
Police Station
Readalot Library
Beachside Boulevard
Stay and Play Park
Squiggly Street
Gym and Swim Recreation Center
Friendly Waves Beach
Duck Duck Goose Pond
School Street

5

Stuart J. Murphy

Percy Gets Upset

Emotional Skills: Dealing with Frustration

Stuart J. Murphy's

I See I Learn

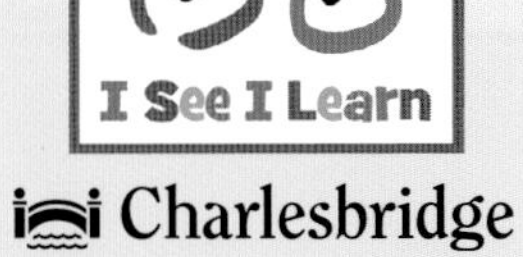

Percy looked everywhere.
"I can't find my other shoe," he said.
"Keep looking," said his mommy.
"It's time to go over to Freda's to play."

Percy stamped his foot. He was **frustrated**.

Where's my shoe?
I can't find it! I can't find it! I can't find it!

"**Calm down**," said his mommy.
"Here it is, right under the chair."

Percy and Freda played hide-and-seek.
Percy's mommy came to the gate.
"We have to go home now, Percy," she said.
"It's almost time for dinner."

Percy scowled. He was **grouchy**.

I want to play!
I won't go! I won't go!

"Percy, try to **stop and think**," said his mommy.
"You can play with Freda again tomorrow."

When they got home,
Percy's daddy had dinner ready.
"Look at the nice meal I made," he said.
"Let's sit down and eat."

Percy put his hands on his hips. He was **cranky**.

I don't want to!
I'm not hungry!
I'm not hungry!

"**Take a deep breath**," said his daddy.
"Then try a few bites. Good food is good for you."

Percy finally ate his meal.
Before bed his daddy read him a funny story.
Then his mommy called,
"It's time to go to sleep, Percy."

Percy crossed his arms. He was **angry**.

I want to stay up!
I'm not tired! I'm not tired!

"You're really upset, Percy,"
said his mommy.
"Do you want to **talk about it**?"

"I just want to stay up," sputtered Percy.
"It's late," said his daddy as he tucked him in.

"Let's **count to ten** together," said his mommy. "Maybe you'll feel better in the morning."

By the time they got to nine, Percy's eyes were starting to close.

The next morning Percy woke up early.
He quietly made his way down the hall.
Then he leaped into the kitchen.
"Guess what?" Percy shouted.

“What?” asked his daddy.
“Tell us,” said his mommy.

Percy smiled. He was **happy**.

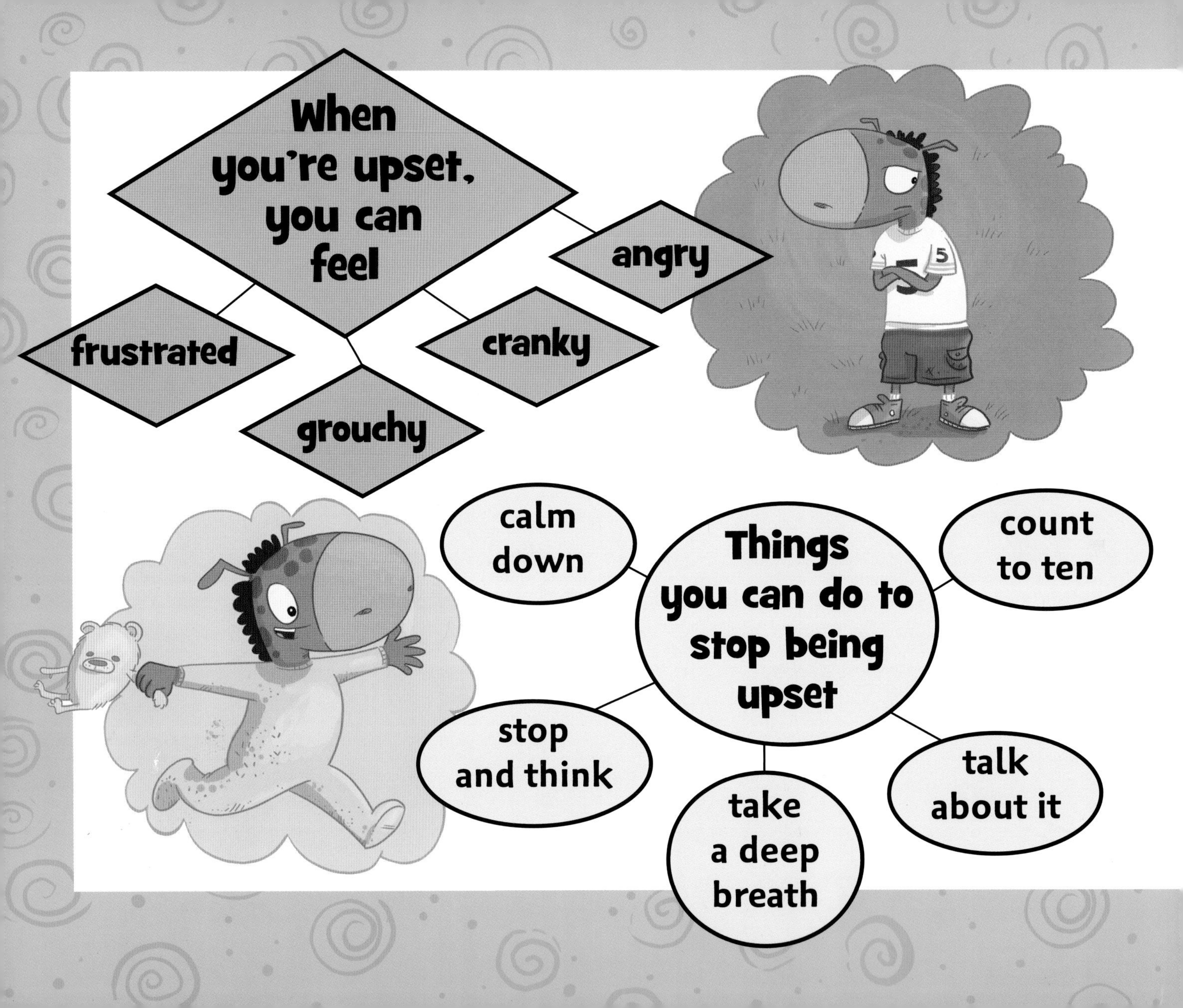
When you're upset, you can feel
angry
cranky
frustrated
grouchy
Things you can do to stop being upset
calm down
count to ten
stop and think
take a deep breath
talk about it

A Closer Look

1. What do **you** do when you're upset?
2. What helps you feel better when you're frustrated or angry?
3. Draw a picture of how you feel when you're grumpy.
4. Draw a picture of how you like to feel.

A Note About Visual Learning and Young Children

Visual Learning describes how we gather and process information from illustrations, diagrams, graphs, symbols, photographs, icons, and other visual models. Long before children can read—or even speak many words—they are able to assimilate visual information with ease. By the time they reach pre-kindergarten age (3–5), they are accomplished visual learners.

I SEE I LEARN™ books build on this natural talent, using inset pictures, diagrams, and highlighted words to help reinforce lessons conveyed through simple stories. The series covers social, emotional, health and safety, and cognitive skills.

Percy Gets Upset focuses on dealing with frustration, an emotional skill. Developing strategies for managing anger, such as taking a deep breath and counting to ten, helps children calm down and feel better.

When you're not upset, you have more fun!

Stuart